DATE DUE

MAY 2 1			
MAR 1 0 1998			
MAR 1 8 1998			
APR 2 8 1998			
SEP 2 9 1998			
NOV 2 4 1998			
DEC 8 1998			
JAN 2 6 1999			
FEB 0 9 1999			
FEB 2 3 1999			
APR 1 3 1999			

MANDARINS AND MARIGOLDS

A Child's Journey through Color

For a free color catalog describing Gareth Stevens' list of high-quality books, call 1-800-542-2595 (USA) or 1-800-461-9120 (Canada). Gareth Stevens' Fax: (414) 225-0377.

— For Fabulous Felix

Library of Congress Cataloging-in-Publication Data
Wallis, Diz.
    Mandarins and marigolds : a child's journey through color / written and illustrated by Diz Wallis. -- North American ed.
      p. cm.
    Summary: A curious boy explores the many colors in his house and the world around him.
    ISBN 0-8368-1391-X
    [1. Color--Fiction.]   I. Title.   *97-51*
PZ7.W159365Man 1995
[E]--dc20   95-16598

North American edition first published in 1995 by
Gareth Stevens Publishing
1555 North RiverCenter Drive, Suite 201
Milwaukee, Wisconsin 53212, USA

This edition licensed by Ragged Bears Limited,
Ragged Appleshaw, Andover, Hampshire SP11 9HX.
Text and illustration © 1995 by Diz Wallis.

Printed in Mexico

1 2 3 4 5 6 7 8 9 99 98 97 96 95

MANDARINS AND MARIGOLDS

A Child's Journey through Color

Written & Illustrated
by **Diz Wallis**

Gareth Stevens Publishing
MILWAUKEE

Once, on a gray and drizzly day, I asked my father where the colors had gone. He said, "The rain has washed them all away. Which do you miss most?"

I closed my eyes to think, then whispered, "blue."
"Ah, blue," he said, and with a pen he drew a blue balloon
to chase the clouds away.

"I wish you blue," he said, "that's bluer than a blue jay's eye, a floating, dreaming, china blue." And all at once I saw blue glass, blue flowers, and a blue, blue sky — a blue that went

on forever. But as I watched in wonder, a yellow bird
distracted me as it sang beside a garden gate.

Through the garden gate I saw a mandarin in yellow silk, picking lemons from a tree. Behind him on a string flew a

newly painted Chinese kite. But the color was still wet, and
blue and yellow ran together making a glorious green.

11

Moss sprang up around my feet, and tiny emerald
frogs leapt into an aqua pool. All the world began
to swim.

12

Then I heard my mother say, "Get out of there; you'll catch a cold. Better come in and warm yourself with red."

Then I was with Mother, making bright red bubbling jam
over an open fire, in a copper pan, in a kitchen that smelled

like strawberries. I looked deep into the glowing coals and thought I saw a marigold.

From the embers there arose a lady in an orange dress, with glowing, flowing, flaming hair, carrying tangerines and

marigolds in a basket on her head. She smiled and beckoned
me to follow her.

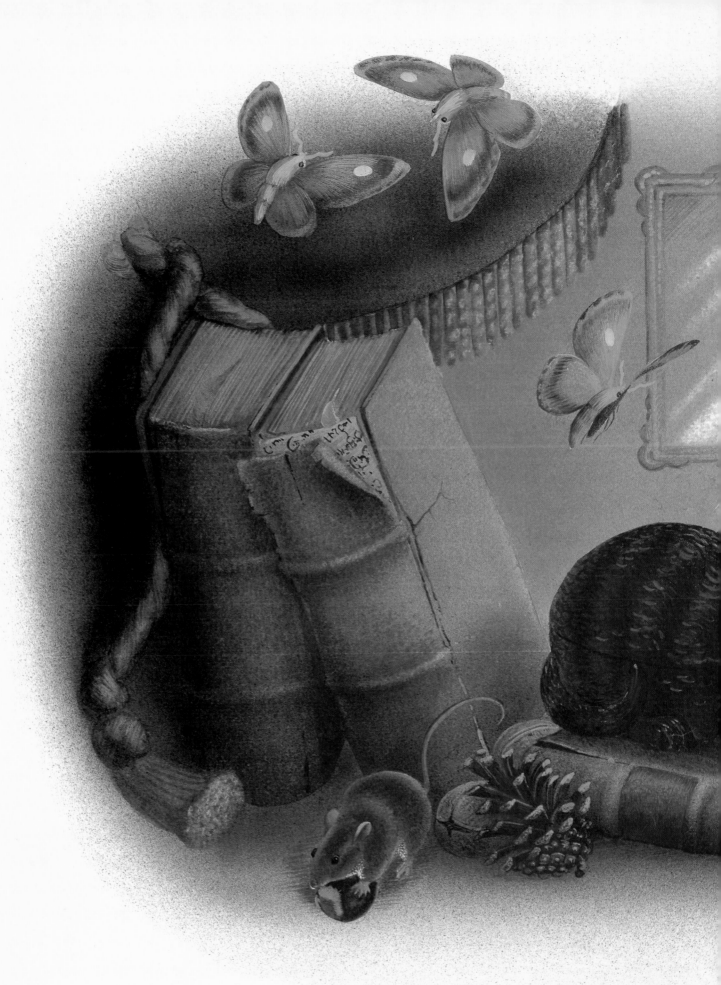

She led me to a brown room inhabited by moths and mice.
The wood revealed the work of worms, and ancient books

shedding their leather bindings. Here the lady disappeared
into a sunny shaft of light, leaving me with only a key.

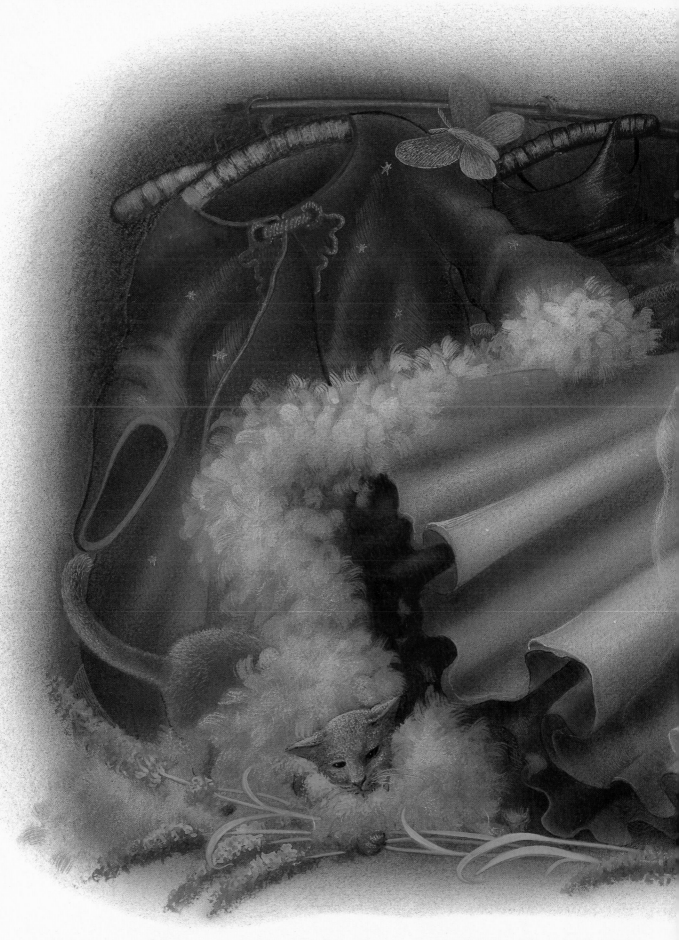

The key opened a wardrobe door. I stepped inside and hid
behind the swirling skirts of a violet gown while a gray cat

hunted and then caught a feather boa. The door banged
shut and night closed in on me.

"It's so dark. I'm scared," I cried. Then my father tossed a
coin into the indigo air. It became a silver moon, shedding

light upon a land where white owls swooped and weasels ran until the eastern sky grew pink.

Dawn broke, and all the world began to blush. Swans rose
from misty lakes, pink as flamingos. Even the trees looked

flushed, and cobwebs hung like cotton candy across the bushes. Then I saw a glint of gold.

I stepped up to take a closer look. Above the honeycomb,
I found a gold ring a swan had dropped, and other golden

treasure, too. I felt my father touch my hand. "Look," he said, "the sun's coming out, and there's a rainbow with it."

It was true. An arc of color leapt across the Earth from
morning to night. And when all trace of rain was gone,

a bright sun shone in a blue, blue sky — a clear blue, a
dreaming blue, a blue that went on forever.